Bad girls, wicked women; lecherous, treacherous villainesses; hedonistic harlots, and plain old-fashioned bunny-boiling temptresses.

Immerse yourself in a feast of delectable depravity with these eight blackly humorous tales, spanning the familiar gothic grimoire of murder, lust and revenge with rapacious relish.

Lascivious lesbians, manipulative mad-women and gruesome gold-diggers are just a few of the bad girls that you'll meet in this fast-paced anthology, which proves beyond all reasonable doubt that the female of the species is definitely more deadly than the male.

BAD GIRLS

Second Edition 2017

Published in the UK, USA and Europe by
Max Publishing

All rights reserved. No part of this publication may be reproduced, stored in a retrieval system or recorded by any means without prior written permission from the publisher. The right of Max Scratchmann to be identified as the author of this work has been asserted by him in accordance with the Copyright, Designs and Patents Act 1988.

© Copyright Max Scratchmann 2010 & 2017

ISBN 978-1545086834

A CIP record for this book is available from the British Library

This book is provided subject to the condition that it shall not, by way of trade or otherwise, be lent, re-sold, hired out, or otherwise circulated without the publisher's prior consent in any form of binding or cover other than that in which it is published and without a similar condition including this condition being imposed on the subsequent purchaser.

Acknowledgments

All the stories in this anthology were written in the late 1980s. **Shhhhhh!** and **Ash** were originally published in *Alfred Hitchcock's Mystery Magazine* and **Poppy** and **Meatburgers** in *Knave Magazine*. **Laura** and **Adrianne** were both unpublished in their own time; and **Claire** and **The Hut** are reconstructions from two unpublished fragments from the same period.

1 2 3 4 5 6 7 8 9

BAD GIRLS

8 NOIR STORIES

Max Scratchmann

Max Publishing

BAD GIRLS

Let us live, my Lesbia, and let us love, and let us reckon all the murmurs of more censorious old men as worth one farthing.

Catullus
84 - 54 BC

ADRIANNE

At thirteen we had been lovers, Adrianne and I. Two children who had always fought like cat and dog briefly in harmony for six pubescent months. And now, almost thirty years later, nothing seemed to have changed. I did not want her but she was my cousin, my blood, and she clung to me. While she was alive.

I had not seen her for well over twenty years. She having married some local accountant-cum-broker in our hometown while I had fled south to the anonymity of London. Or so I thought. Then, a matter of days before my forty-third birthday, a letter had clung gastropod-like to my mat and there was something familiar, sticky-sweet and nauseating, about the fawning tilt of the handwriting. Violet ink on faintly scented lilac paper.

It had to be her. And it was.

It seemed that fate was against me. She was in London. Resident. Streets away. Kevin, the husband, had inveigled his fat, slippery arse into some wonderful yuppie job and they had arrived. Sickeningly close to me. Like a bad penny or a portrait in the attic, hanging onto a familial thread that did not exist, suffocating me already with invitations to a dinner party that never happened.

Because Kevin got himself killed.

So, instead of meeting over candles and some newly-purchased Heal's dining set, our reunion took place in the sombre maroon and grey outer offices of the local undertaker's shop. A banal joining of two lost souls under the ministrations of one Frazer Salter: a large effusive man who looked as if he should have been a sales rep for Callard & Bowser, and who flipped the plastic pages in his vision-book of coffins with all the solemnity of a man showing the latest catalogue of toffee tins.

And, just as when we were children, Adrianne went to pieces and left all the arrangements in my capable hands. Looking at her, a small quivering heap of blonde hair and tears, she didn't seem to have changed at all. Her hair was being dyed now, of course, to cover the first strands of grey, and there were bigger bags under her eyes than I remembered. Also a trace of crows' feet here and there, and her old haunted look had become more pronounced. But that was it. She was essentially the same old Adrianne. Adrianne the cry baby. Adrianne the motherless waif. Adrianne who had delighted in standing up in the bath and peeing in a golden arc. Adrianne who used to cry if I didn't let her choose every game we were to play. Adrianne who coveted my first dark strands of pubic hair while she thrust her own smooth crotch into my face.

Smothering me.

I honestly didn't know if I loved her or hated her and she was dead before I had the chance to find out. But she was the same old Adrianne to the last. Adrianne my golden-haired darling who left me tangled in a web of blood as her extra special parting gift.

* * * * *

The world, that is, *my* world, was swimming in front of me and I walked through water. And Adrianne clung to me, pulling me down. We were being ushered out of the office by the undertaker's wife. A thin dried-blade-of-grass sort of a woman. A tubercular Wicked Witch of the West. And Adrianne was crying. No, Adrianne was treating the whole street to The Works. A neurotic Bette Davis in *Of Human Bondage* with shades of *Baby Jane*. Like when she was small and she'd been to the dentist's for a filling and cried and cried all night.

And then, suddenly, as we turned into the street, the tears stopped and the fear took over.

"Margaret," she whispered, clutching my arm like a tourniquet, "I'm in trouble. Don't take me to your house. They'll be watching there. You know this place, can you make us vanish so we can talk?"

And what the hell was I supposed to do? Yet this was no act, no well-worn Adrianne ploy for attention. I could feel the urgency in her voice, smell the fear in her sweat. But this was London in the eighties, not Chicago in some grainy black and white thirties' film. But I did what I could. Did it Woolrich. Did it Cain. Took her to look at a shop window, pointed, discussed, then suddenly doubled back on our tracks and ducked down an alley. Hurried down a busy loading street, then quickly darted under the red brick arches of the old Peabody estate. Criss-crossing the footpaths to the stairs that were almost completely engulfed by thorny bushes. Like Sleeping Beauty's castle. Scurrying down the worn concrete to the underworld and then suddenly out in the cold autumn sunshine of the main artery again.

We quickly crossed the London Road and spun through the revolving doors and vanished down the rabbit hole of the Art Nouveau bowels of the Horniman Museum. And there, over delft cups of strong tea in the tiny basement café, my arm still pulsating from her blood-stopping grip while endless parties of school children shuffled past us, she unfolded the full gory details of what she had gotten herself into.

BAD GIRLS

It ran like something out a B movie. A very bad one.

The rotund Kevin had not come down to any waiting job. A second-rate accountant at best, he had been floundering for the last two decades, yet had managed to "survive" – in style, if the labels on her garments were anything to go by – by handling the books of a local "business syndicate".

And she had always known. Tacitly approved. Been turned on by the frisson of risk. The kick of criminality. And they had been well paid for their silence. Until Kevin, she *said*, had decided to branch out on a little flutter of his own. A little something on the side to sweeten an already overflowing pot.

It was poetic, really. I could see the whole sorry tale playing out in my head like some embarrassing silent melodrama. The inept amateur virtually penning his own suicide note to his rapacious doll-wife as he plunges head-first into some pathetic venture predestined to failure, using, of course, the money of his merciless employers.

Clasping an anxious hand to his forehead, Kevin's speech card appears:

"Darling, we are undone! What shall we do?"

Cut to Adrianne, complete with Mary Pickford wig, all

innocence and kohl-black eye-make-up, a decorative tear running down her flawless cheek as she speaks:

"Why, we'll dump it all on Margaret, of course. Now kiss me, you fool!"

And now the portly Kevin was dead. Officially the victim of a hit-and-run driver. A driver who, strangely, the local gendarmes didn't seem too perturbed about locating, or about asking why he'd reversed over Kevin's fat flailing body and then run him over again, while Adrianne cowered in the shadows of a shop doorway, a torrent of hot urine gushing down her shivering thigh as she came face-to-face with her own rapidly-approaching mortality.

* * * * *

But now everything was going to be alright. Margaret was here. Margaret would kiss it better. Like she'd always done before. Except that Margaret was fresh out of ideas, Margaret didn't have a clue. So I sent her off to hide. Gave her money and told her to disappear. Put her on a train and never saw her again.

* * * * *

She lasted three days. Then there was a fire in a cheap boarding house in Margate. A faulty electric heater in the attic regions of a quiet off-season hotel that turned into a hungry inferno which consumed everything in its path.

And so she was gone, and yet, I feared, not soon to be forgotten.

* * * * *

They left me alone for three long weeks. Left me alone with my thoughts and fears. Left me to lie sleepless and tell myself it had all been a bad dream. I could have run, but I didn't. I lived in splendid isolation. I didn't even have a bank account or a credit card. No commitments. No traces. I had built myself a comfortable, if uninspiring, nest and I had no intention of leaving it. The ball was in their court. Let them come, I thought defiantly.

And then the doorbell rang.

I had lived in London for over twenty years. I had no casual acquaintances and certainly no friends. And the gas meter had been read. Besides, no-one ever called at this particular Miss Havisham's mansion unless they had to.

Rising, I told myself it was the Jehovah's Witnesses but I knew it wouldn't be.

It was the police.

In all good stories the heroine always makes A Mistake. I made mine now. I had never trusted the police. Never thought I would be glad to see them. But when the WPC at my door said she wanted a few words about the death of my cousin I stood back and invited the vampire in. I was glad to see her. Glad that everything was coming out into the open at last. That was my mistake. I should have known that Adrianne would never have left me in a mess where anything was as it seemed. And that a uniform is nothing more than some pieces of cloth.

"You're Mrs Kelvendale's only living relative, is that correct, Miss Cunningham?" she asked from the depths of my settee.

I nodded and she made a little note in her book, folded her arms and smiled. That familiar police smile. Obsequious and insulting. The unique police blend, stirring dim chords of memory in me. A group of us at a church-hall dance that had ended in a fight. Two coxcombed Teds strutting and threatening on the dance floor. Spilled drinks and screaming. A ballet of aggression, full of the sound and fury... But the boys in blue had been called. A stocky WPC herding all us girls into the Ladies' loo to give us her pep talk on The Wrong Kind of Boy. I was how old? Fifteen? Sixteen?

And then she lovingly patted us all down for concealed weapons. And all my life I keep brushing against women who want to pat me down.

But there was something not quite right about this one. Something that didn't quite gel. Dare I say that I didn't like the way she looked at me?

"You were aware, were you not, Miss Cunningham," she was saying in the bored sing-song voice of police training school, "that your cousin owed money when she died. Quite a substantial sum, in fact."

I winced as I felt her verbal punch somewhere around my stomach. This was no routine enquiry. I opened my mouth to speak but no words came.

She saw my distress and smiled. Wet her lips daintily with a tiny pink cat's tongue. I watched it curl over a pretty little moustache dusted with an icing of face powder.

"Please don't be distressed," she said and pretended a smile. There was a slight trace of the Scottish in her accent. Many years back. Edinburgh, I thought.

She was still talking. "This is not what you'd call official police business," she said, slightly mockingly, pausing to let the penny drop.

I sighed. So this was it then. No thugs at my door. No tragic accidents. Just a single slightly apologetic lady PC earning some pin money in her spare time. She could have been working for Avon. She acted as if she thought she was.

"The firm I represent, Miss Cunningham, doesn't write off debts," she was saying, going through the pre-learned script she had recited a hundred times before, "I'm afraid we *always* collect."

She said the last line slowly, patiently, as if she was stressing an awkward clause in an insurance policy.

I wondered if I should just hit her, snap her fat neck like a chicken. But she she matched me pound for pound, inch for inch. It wouldn't be clean. And I liked clean.

"But I don't have that kind of money," I remonstrated, buying time, "God, I haven't even seen the woman in over twenty years!"

She silenced me with a weary inclination of her hand. She had heard this routine many times before and was bored with it. The tongue performed its little trick again and she began to speak once more.

"Miss Cunningham," she sighed, "we *know* what you have and don't have. We always check on our clients *before* we make a request."

Her tone was patronising now, defensive of the professionalism of her employers. I shrugged and she had the cheek to look wounded.

"*Please*, Miss Cunningham," she said reproachfully, "we are not monsters. We realise that none of this is any fault of yours. It's just a case of family obligation, and we all have families, don't we? Now, you have a good job and your overheads are low. We're quite happy to let you settle this little matter by instalments."

I was stunned by the mundaneness of it all. "Instalments?" I repeated blandly, for want of something better to say.

She smiled brightly and snapped her notebook shut. The deal was done and now it was time to play. I contemplated hitting her again, picking up the heavy brass table lamp and bashing her head in. But they would find me again, maybe not tomorrow or the next day, but eventually. I sighed wearily and stayed where I was. I had lost a battle, the war was yet to be won.

"So who do I pay these *instalments* to?" I asked sarcastically. It was wasted on her.

"To me. You won't ever meet my employers. I'll call in person once a month. Or weekly, if you prefer. Just remember that it must be cash, though, no substitutes…"

Her voice trailed off as her tone changed from business-like to sly. What was she trying to say?

"Of course," I said vacantly, trying to work out the change of mood. I hadn't liked her when she had been brusque. I liked her even less now.

It had begun to get dark while we had been talking and my Indian brass lamp did nothing to brighten up the now gloomy room. Instead it threw long dancing shadows onto the walls and made the place look darker. She was looking at me intently but I couldn't make out her expression and I was just about to speak when she got up to stare out of the window, suddenly absorbed in the rapidly descending dusk.

"You live here alone?"

"Yes."

"No boyfriend? Never married?"

"No," I said cautiously. This was very thin ice.

But obviously I had answered her questions correctly. Three fat juicy plums had lined up and the jackpot was due to spill tumbling onto the floor.

"This needn't be the ordeal you think it's going to be," she said softly, without looking at me. "We could be friends..."

I was glad that I was sitting down. I think that I might have fallen over if I hadn't been.

"What sort of friends?" I heard myself ask.

Silence. Long and dark. Dust floating in the soft beams of lamplight. Then.

"Intimate friends."

"This is so sudden," I said.

She looked at me for a moment, an insecure expression on her face, then took my facetiousness at face value. Everything was tidy now. The day's business had been concluded and the lackey had organised her cut. Her pound of flesh.

"And when do we start being *friends*?" I asked, but I knew the answer to that one before she opened her mouth.

The tongue licked more powder off her hairy upper lip.

"No time like the present..." she said quietly.

BAD GIRLS

* * * * *

The hallway that led to my bedroom was lucky if it was ten feet long, but today it seemed endless and smelt of damp and old wardrobes. There was no light. The bulb had fused weeks ago and I had never bothered to replace it. The policewoman led the way. I didn't even know her name. It was like going down to the cell blocks.

Turning to embrace me at my bedroom door. Roughly. Urgently. A slight taint of tobacco on her breath. Her hair hinting of the smoky autumn evening. Her kiss vibrant. Clinging. She cups my breasts. Hard. Her breath hot in my ear as she whispers: "First time?"

And all I could see was miles of unending corridor. Not mine, but in my grandmother's house when I was small. The steam white from the open bathroom door. Wet on the cracked white wall tiles. And Adrianne, like a boy, peeing in the bath, a glittering golden arc steaming into the greenish water. And it was so cold and dark in the hallway and I could hear my granny doing the dishes in the kitchen. Shhh, Adrianne, she'll hear. And her breath is hot and her lips wet. And, yes, Adrianne, you're my bestest friend, of course I love you. Put your hand there if you want to.

The bedroom was dim. Pink in the glow of the electric fire. The bedcover snowy-white. She undressed me deftly with a practiced hand. A butcher expertly skinning a freshly slaughtered rabbit, my naked body white on the white candlewick and I could still hear Adrianne sobbing because her tooth hurt and the policewoman was naked too. Did *I* undress her? She was pressing my hands to her breasts, her stomach, lower, pushing her lips on my lips, raping me with her tongue. Sucking at my nipples, forcing them erect, demanding reactions.

And it wasn't repulsive and it didn't thrill me. It was empty. Just empty. Like fingering my own reflection. We were peas in a pod. Sisters. Clones from the same mould. Same build. Same colouring. What did she see in me? Herself?

* * * * *

Later, as she lay cradled in my arms and the darkness crept around us, she slept softly. I absently stroked her hair and hated her, and the furniture seemed to orbit around us in the flecked air. But as the dust burned in the heater I didn't think about Adrianne. Not now. Not in the quiet time. The loving time.

I thought about Peter.

* * * * *

I am eighteen. I am not what most boys consider attractive.

Rather solid of build. Thick around the waist. Acne. Lifeless dark hair. Monroe was dead but gentlemen still seemed to prefer blondes. Or at least Adrianne. But not Peter. Peter was different. Peter was tall and shy. Peter read books when the other boys played football in the mud and rain. And Peter had no time for empty-headed Adrianne.

Peter wanted me.

* * * * *

I appraise her sleeping form. She is incredibly like me. Her breasts are slightly larger, her stomach a little firmer, her body more hirsute.

I kiss her softly, crooning to her. The room is very dark.

* * * * *

Peter wanted me. Wanted someone to read *Lady Chatterley* to. Wanted someone to cherish in fields, to make hay with while the sun shone. And I was more than willing. That summer day in the old meadow, miles from town. It was hot and he had taken his shirt off. I was hot too, wanted to feel the sun on my back. I don't remember who took my blouse off but I was ashamed of my worn old white bra. He took that off.

Girls at school had said it that hurt like hell the first time but not for me. He worshipped me. Worshipped my body. And he was so tender. So caring. He threaded wild flowers through my pubic hair like the girl in the book and kissed me and told me he loved me.

I had never been so happy in all my life.

*   *   *   *   *

She moans softly in her slumber as I stroke her breast and I can feel the same tingle I felt when Adrianne's curious fingers first travelled down my abdomen.

I caress the pillow with my free hand. I can feel a dark river welling up and pulsating somewhere in the depths of my body.

*   *   *   *   *

It is a Sunday evening in late September. I have been out with Peter all day, all beautiful day. My mother stands waiting for me at the red-brick arch of our doorway. Her arms are folded and her eyes are those of one betrayed. My mother and I live alone together in the domicile the council has generously provided for us. My father is dead. Or dying. We don't know. Alcoholic, you know, very sad. He left before I was old enough to know he existed. Mum says she does not miss him. Mum has me, she says. Mum has always made sure I had plenty to eat, a roof over my head, kind arms to hold me. And today something is wrong. Today is the day for the big showdown.

But I say nothing. I leave the ball in her court. That is my style.

My mother holds up a disgusting-looking pink thing. It looks like the aftermath of an abortion. And it smells rank. I realise with a jolt that it is a spent condom. Now I know why it is a showdown.

My mother has found it in the dustbin. I told him to flush it down the toilet but he wouldn't listen. Now it is telling tales. I wait patiently for my mother to read me the riot act. I can feel the black river of hate pulsing against my innards.

But Mamma Bear does not rant and rave, she does not scream.

She cries.

Big, fat, wet tears. Plopping down onto the ancient lino in the kitchen. Crying like a baby. Fawning over me. Sucking at my soul. How could I do this to her? Clinging. I was all she had, how could I? I was fat. I had spots. She had thought I would be a safe bet. But I must never leave her. I wouldn't, would I? Mummy loved me so much. So very, very much.

BAD GIRLS

She waited for me to say my lines. Yes, Mummy, you're my bestest friend...

* * * * *

I squeeze her breast and feel the nipple stiffen as she grinds closer to me. Clinging. My bestest friend.

* * * * *

The river bursts its banks. The black water turns to red. It is time to say goodbye to best friends.

My mother is a small and fragile woman. She has spent the last eighteen years perfecting being frail and sickly. But my how she kicks and spits when I try to strangle her.

Eventually I grab her by the hair and smash her head against the kitchen wall. On the rough part where the geyser used to be.

It is a terrible mess for me to find.

* * * * *

I place the pillow quickly over the sleeping policewoman's face and hold it there, my hands inside the slip so that her nails won't mark me. But she's a good girl. She goes peacefully.

* * * * *

My mother's death was a terrible shock to me. I had to have quite a lengthy sojourn in hospital to get over it while the police searched in vain for her killer. Peter stayed by my side throughout it all. It seemed like he was practically living in the hospital corridor. It wasn't until I was due to return home and he said that he was coming with me that I realised he *had* been living there.

It seemed that his mother had found out about his rural flower arranging habits and Peter-Peter had been promptly expelled from his comfortable nest. So he wanted to climb into his bestest friend's.

But inside every homeless Peter there's an Adrianne fighting to get out.

* * * * *

I dress myself carefully in the policewoman's clothes. All of them. Even her tights and knickers, although it makes my stomach turn. I put the pillow back and make her more comfortable. Put the local paper in her hands. She almost looks pretty, sitting cosy and contented in bed like that with my favourite cup by her bedside.

BAD GIRLS

A bit like Adrianne in that dreary Margate hotel room.

I put two fifty-pence-pieces in the meter so that the electric fire will stay on for a while longer. Then, picking up her handbag, I slip quietly out into the night, the draught from the closing door sending the newspaper fluttering towards the gleaming red bars.

* * * * *

But Peter did the right thing after all. The poor fellow died in a tragic accident. Fell asleep beside the fire with some of his paperback books lying too close and a stray ember must have ignited the lot. He wasn't used to fending for himself, I suppose. There wasn't very much left of him by the time they put the fire out.

* * * * *

The piece about my death in the local paper wasn't much of an obituary but I don't mind. A couple of paragraphs about the blaze and a whole feature on the new development the landlord was going to build on the site. And working for the police isn't too bad, either. I had to put in for compassionate leave and a transfer after being the last person to see poor Miss Cunningham alive, of course. But, all in all, things are good at my new district office. And the money from my spare time job is very good too.

Of course, the 'clients' all know I'm not her, but now they don't have to be "intimate friends" any longer, so they're happy too.

Mother always said things have a way of working out if you just let them.

ASH

Ashley had sworn that he'd come back. It was the last thing he'd said as Wishart pushed him out of the window, and although Wishart wasn't the superstitious type, he'd had him cremated anyway. Just in case.

But it seemed that he needn't have worried. Ashley seemed quite content to stay under his rose tree in the Garden of Remembrance and never did the soft swish of ashy feet sound in Wishart's hallway or pace past his bolted door. Until he began to court Elinor again.

Now Elinor had been Wishart's girl at university back in '82, but of recent years she had been more taken with the charms of elder brother Ashley and his rancid Porsche. Even though the car phone kept ringing every time they went out together.

But it hadn't been any good. Elinor had fallen for the £135,000 per annum and the second house in Brighton, and Wishart had been forced to do the sporting and gentlemanly thing and push his sod of a brother out of the window. Which hadn't been at all easy.

However, once he'd finally managed to spin a yarn good enough to lure the lardy lout round to his flat in Battersea, it had been quite easy to convince him that there was a wounded bird on the ledge and that he, Wishart, was too scared to go out and get it. After that it had been more or less plain sailing. Less, in the sense that Ashley had clung on tenaciously to his fat life, and Wishart had had to be *very* careful just how he whacked his brother's grasping little fingers with the walking stick; but more when the deed was done and the police and public had swallowed – hook, line and sinker – his story of Ashley's fatal accident whilst trying to save the life of a tiny fledgling sparrow. The fat greaseball had even made it to the front page of the local paper. Still, Wishart was cautious.

But his fears had seemed groundless until that Fatal First Night he brought Elinor back to his flat. They had been to a concert at the South Bank – Elinor's first public appearance, as the saying goes, since the death of her fiancé – and she had confided to him over coffee that she really needed to get out more and that she was glad to have old friends like him to rely on.

Wishart's heart sang. And then sank as he saw the delicate flakes of ash fluttering against the window pane.

Wishart froze. Despite the central heating. But there was no denying it. Snowflake-cute and bobbing like a syncopated defector from *Fantasia,* it fluttered and pirouetted against the neon-pierced velvet of the night sky. Ash. Ashley's ash.

Wishart pulled himself together, drew the curtains and closed his mind.

But he slipped up three weeks later, when, bowled over with excitement because she'd let him kiss her cheek when he escorted her home the previous night, he was too busy putting on his kid gloves to notice that he'd left the living room window open and the thick velvet drapes ajar.

And it had been quite a descent from Seventh Heaven when one moment they'd been kissing passionately on the settee and the next some gentle gossamer-floating-thing had lightly stroked his cheek and drifted daintily onto his lap.

He'd let out a yell. No, let's be honest here. He'd screamed his head off and then cried like a baby. And it had taken the puzzled Elinor almost ten minutes to finally quieten him down, and another half hour to get back to where they had left off on the couch.

But the Grand Finale came two weeks later when she rose from the settee, and, taking his hand, smiled her Little Girl Lost smile and asked coyly where the bedroom was. And with

Wishart's heart doing rapid-succession press-ups, they glided through the open door and floated down onto the snowy white bedspread which was, of course, covered in a fine white, flour-lite dusting of – altogether now – ash.

It was the straw the camel dreads and Wishart went berserk, screaming and wailing and clutching at Elinor's skirt as she tried to comfort him. And then, of course, the fool went and blurted out the whole sordid story.

But she took it calmly enough and patted and 'there-there'd him at all the appropriate places, and when he was done she even went and got her handbag for tissues to dab his eyes with. And they sat there like that for a long time, while he sobbed and she crooned fairy tales (yes, fairy tales) in his ear to console him.

"There now, there now," she soothed. "Dry your eyes and Elinor will tell you a story. A sad story that happened long, long ago. Listen...

"Once upon a time there lived a Beautiful Maiden who loved a Scholar, but, as The Scholar was never likely to rise beyond the village of Battersea, the Maiden decided to marry the Fat Prince, confident that once she had his riches some misfortune would befall him and free her. However, unbeknownst to her, The Scholar, inflamed with jealousy, went and slew the Fat Prince before the Maiden could lay claim to his loot. So can you guess what the Maiden did to the silly Scholar when he finally spilled the beans, Wishart?"

But there was no glittering star prize behind the red and gold dappled curtains for solving this particular little conundrum, and the disgustingly convenient little lady-gun with its mother-of-pearl handle that she slipped out of her bag gave the game away long before the roar of the explosion seared his eardrums.

In fact, the report was so loud that, under normal circumstances, grumpy old Mr Peterson from next door would have been shuffling over in his carpet slippers to moan about the noise. But, as he was sitting at his kitchen table writing an irate letter to the factory at the bottom of the road at the time, he missed the whole show.

Their damned incinerator had developed the filthy habit of blowing ash through his front windows and he wasn't standing for it. After all, if everybody just threw their ash around unchecked, it wouldn't be long before people were suffocating in the damn stuff and dropping dead because of it. And, believe you me, *he* wasn't going to end up being found dead in his living room after fighting in the last war for a cleaner place to live.

But, unfortunately, The Fates were working from a different script, and, even as his indignant pen flew over the Basildon

Bond, Elinor was easing up the latch on his door and creeping stealthily up behind him.

Not that she had any *real* need to get rid of the old fool, of course, because he'd heard nothing and didn't know she existed anyway. But Elinor was a methodical worker and just liked to be sure all the loose ends were tidy.

After all, that was the trouble with the world today, wasn't it? You never could be sure that some maniac with a gun wasn't going to walk in off the street and mow down two innocent, unconnected people. Or even, for that matter, that a truck would career blindly off the road and strike a hurrying girl because the driver got dust in his eyes. Or maybe even ash?

LAURA

A cold wind was blowing rain like iced needles in off the sea on the afternoon we buried Laura.

There were five of us: the vicar, who was a stranger, old and cold, rushing through the *ashes to ashes*, his reddened fingers aching to get back to the comfort of his fireplace; two miscellaneous old crones from the village in mothball-smelling weeds that had been brought out for the occasion, although they had hardly known her; I, who had loved her, dry-eyed and numb with cold and loss, and, lastly, her face wet with tears and body heaving with sobs, Lavinia Devondale, who had killed her.

We rained cinder-like clumps of frost-hardened soil onto the lid of her dark polished-wood coffin and suddenly it was over. The vicar mumbled something unintelligible to me and hurried away, already dreaming of toast and the evening paper by his roaring fire. The two crones kissed my corpse-cold cheeks with cracked lips and wove away through the zig-zag of old tombstones, the sea-facing ones almost illegible after centuries of salt and wind had slowly erased the ancient names of their occupants. Caleb Armstrong. Abraham Bell. Carpenter. Builder. Master Mariner. All stood for nothing now, just fading names being washed away by the rage of a mighty sea that foamed and tossed in its grey bed not a hundred yards away.

And what would I put on your epitaph, Laura? Lover? Friend? Life? How long will the sea spare your memory, my darling, as you lie here in this cold and brittle bed? And how can I leave you here, alone, with only the long dead for company?

A sound made me turn, and revealed two muffled figures, ragged scarves billowing in the wind, sinister silhouettes against the already purple sky, as what was left of the sun sank into the hungry sea.

"Can we get on, like?" one – I couldn't tell which – asked. So it had come to this. Grief was a coin worth little against a cold grave-digger's desire to finish for the evening and go home.

I nodded assent and dropped my frost-withered blooms into the pit. Goodbye Laura. This is our last farewell and I can't even kiss you. I never left you before without kissing you and now I send you into eternity without the blessing of my lips.

Goodbye, my darling, sleep tight, I'll buy you a beautiful flaxen angel to tower above these lowly mariner's stumps. So that you can be remembered in all your resplendent glory against the setting sun every shimmering summer night, when this now-grey sea runs with molten gold and brings back those nights when you dived and bobbed in the waves like a mermaid, or some sea creature that only took human form to grace my lonely bed at nights, gone by morning.

I turned abruptly as the brittle soil began to rain down on her and walked slowly down the lane and headed for home. Home, the tiny cottage that had been the centre of our universe and our love for over twenty years. When we first came from London, the villagers had thought of us as two spinster sisters, and Laura said there was no harm in that if that's what it made them comfortable to believe. So we never corrected the rumour.

And today, with the fire still unlit and the previous night's ashes still grey and leaden in the grate, it suddenly seemed small and barren, but I felt that even if the fire was roaring there would be no heat or light because the light had gone forever and was lying in the cold grip of the frosty soil at sea's edge. Oh Laura, I miss you so!

Really, the angle of her eyebrows would have said, if she were here. *Won't you ever grow up?* I could see her, clear as day, paintbrush in hand, looking up at me from the pot she was painting, half smiling, half annoyed. Emotions were something Laura never showed. Life was a constant flow of calm for her and my periodic tears and worries never failed to amuse and irritate her simultaneously.

Numbly, I began to sweep out the grate and lay the fire, working methodically, robotically, lighting the paper and listening to the crackle of the sticks as they caught, remembering the sounds of the room when she was here, the long winter evenings when the wind howled and screamed outside and we sat, not talking, Laura busy with her brushes, deftly painting life onto the pots that I had thrown in the small shed outside, turning the ordinary into the magical, converting a replica amphora into an antique with a real history, a dull dish into a fairytale adventure with dark woods full of wolves and goblins giving way to enchanted castles and mazes to wander through and lose yourself in.

Sometimes she would let me put a record on, softly. But usually the only music was the soft stroking of her brush and the gentle caress of the fire as a coal shifted in its fiery bed like a sleeper turning in the night. What did I do all those evenings? My work had been done during the daylight hours. I had sat at the wheel with the moist clay in my hands, spinning out what she asked for like some earthly Rumpelstiltskin; loaded the trays of waiting receptacles into the kiln; stacked the finished pots into the plastic crates kept for the purpose, so she could convert them into the wares that graced our stalls in the markets at Keswick and Cockermouth in the summer months, when our days were spent plying our craft to the tourists who flooded to the area to see where Wordsworth saw his daffodils, and take home a souvenir for the folks back home. Laura always refused to have anything with daffodils or nightingales or Souvenir of the Lakes on our stall, yet it was always us who went home with empty crates, while the models of Wordsworth's house on our neighbours' stalls often accompanied them to market after market.

It was not that there was anything unusual about Laura's art: standard Roman and Greek urns, picture book fairytale scenes on plates and plaques, Pre-Raphaelite maidens and knights in armour. And yet they had a magic that no-one could match. We didn't try to be unique – I had learned my pottery at St Martin's – but Laura was a natural. She was special. Her painting glowed. It was real. You knew that the amphora wasn't Roman, but you believed it was. Somehow she painted on a thousand years of history.

And now I was left alone to try and capture the uncaptureable. The fire was lit, the room was warming, and yet it was lifeless. I could put on Don Giovanni or La Boheme and fill the place with sound and yet there would be nothing. It would be empty, and cold, and dead.

Oh Laura, Laura, Laura.

A knock at the door made my heart pound as adrenaline coursed through my veins. Lavinia, of course. I walked slowly to the door and opened it, my body barring the way, forbidding her entrance.

"I'm going now," she said, her small pinched face tear-stained, the threadbare collar turned up inadequately against the wind outside. I was unmoved. Let the bitch freeze!

I nodded. I had nothing to say to her.

"I'm taking the six o'clock train. I'll be in London by morning. You won't hear from me again."

I nodded again and made to shut the door, but she thrust her thin gloved hand out.

"Elsebeth," she whined, "I'm so *sorry!*"

I shut the door on her and wished I had done that three months ago when she had first showed her pathetic little face there.

Three months. Had it only been three short months for my whole world to dissolve around me? Three months for some *insect* like little Lavinia Devondale to sidle in and destroy what had taken a lifetime to build? Oh Laura, I've been such a fool.

It had been a particularly busy day in late September. The last veins of tourist trade were proving to be rich, and a steady stream of people was coursing past our stall in front of Wordsworth's Cockermouth residence. Laura, as usual, seemed to glide from one to the other, answering questions, giving directions, taking money, all with the same unflappable calm. I, predictably, was harassed, trying desperately to cope with the sea of faces that ebbed and flowed in front of me as the backdrop of red and gold-leaved trees behind them shimmered gently in what threatened to become the first wind of winter.

Then I saw her. A thin pinched face, dismissive of what it saw before it. A face that wasn't going to be lulled into parting with money by the seductive lure of Laura's magic paintbrush. I didn't know *then* why my blood ran cold. I had seen faces like that before. In the tourist trade every coach party had one. So why was this one so terrifying? Because it was a face from the past?

She was gone before I could place her, and although I told myself how silly I was being, I couldn't shake off the feeling of dread that was with me all that day. It felt, somehow, that like the leaves in their shimmering gold on all the trees, the days of my happiness were numbered. And I was proved to be right.

She appeared at our door that night. Laura had gone down to the beach to watch the sunset, although I had declined on the pretence of cooking a meal for us. Her knock was like the knocking in Macbeth that summons the watchers to witness the bloody murder of the king. I opened the door and there she was. Not just Lavinia Devondale but over twenty forgotten years and a lifestyle so far away it almost belonged to another person. And up till now it really had. I didn't have to ask her what she wanted or who she was, I already knew. I only had to discover how *much* she wanted. And, in my bones, I knew it would be a lot, but even then I never guessed just what a lot it really would be.

It began in 1962. Before the Beatles and Carnaby Street and free love and antiwar demonstrations. I was an art student at St Martins. I had a little talent and a wealthy father, so I was entitled to live a bohemian existence. My allowance ran to a flat in Soho, walking distance from Long Acre, and a few modest entertainments like the gods at Covent Garden. I was content, if not happy, until the day I met Laura and she turned my whole life upside down. I suppose, in retrospect, we could have been 'discreet', but we were nineteen and madly in love and discretion was the last thing on our minds. I had heard an altercation in a back alley on my way home one night and, although my normal reaction would have been to flee quickly to my own little nest, I charged in to assist.

I came upon a 'lady of the night', a tall blonde girl about my own age, locked in combat with a beefy little man in his mid-forties and I rushed to her defence. I know now that she had little need of my help and that the cries for assistance had come from her 'assailant' and not from her, but at the time I was a knight on a white charger and she was my damsel in distress. Between us we thrashed the living daylights out of that poor little man and sent him scampering off as if all the devils in hell were after him, which would probably have been the softer option.

We had no formal introductions, we didn't need them, but neither of us were surprised when we spent that night together and were never parted thereafter. We were open about our love, and London, despite what legend would have you believe, did not look kindly on us for it.

We had six weeks of borrowed time before the house of cards tumbled. My landlady gave me notice. "I thought you good girl," she muttered sadly. The art school wrote to my parents and asked them to rebuke me or remove me. I was summoned home. I was a rich man's daughter. Laura had been a prostitute. This foolishness had to end if I were to continue at the art school. When I indicated that I couldn't give two hoots about the college, the real cards were laid on the table before us. Laura could have a named sum and never see me again, an offer she answered with a sniff of contempt, or we could be bought a house, far away, and have a modest annuity to survive on. We would never again show our faces in London and any attempt at contact would cut the financial flow at a stroke. I would no longer be my father's daughter. We accepted and flew on a magic carpet of our own weaving to a life of unchallenged happiness for over two decades, until this chilly September day.

Lavinia had been at art school with me. Like me she had a moderate talent, but no rich father to support her. She had known about our 'scandal' and seeing us all these years later must have seemed like the final reprieve from all those ill-paid commissions from women's magazines and the temp jobs in offices and bars. Lavinia's thin hand wore a neatly darned glove. Her coat was out of date. Life had not been kind to her but she was about to settle up the score. She saw not only the material comfort that my annuity and our success in the tourist trade afforded us, but written in large letters all over our lives was the word "happiness" and *that* she begrudged us. Her expression told me that she would bleed us dry. Her expression did not lie.

I kept it from Laura for ten weeks. Ten weeks of lies and evasions. Ten weeks of secrecy in a relationship where there had never been a closed door. Ten weeks of seeing hurt in her eyes and being powerless to do a thing about it. Ten weeks of hell on earth in our private heaven.

But we couldn't go on as we were, and eventually she found out. The payments to Lavinia were making inroads into our capital and I could only conceal it for so long. She challenged me with it one chilly December morning, when a bright winter sun was streaming through the frosty kitchen window, and I collapsed in a heap on the cold flags and told her everything.

She looked at me with sheer incredulity, mixed with amazement, for at least sixty seconds after I had finished and then said, very quietly, "I will not live as anybody's slave," and walked out of the door without another word. It was to be the last sight I would have of her.

The news of her death came a day later and I just sat there numb with shock at the enormity of what she had done. Oh Laura, Laura, Laura.

And now it was all over. The death, the funeral, the blackmailer's remorse. Absently, I put the guard on the fire and began to straighten the room, working methodically to keep my hands occupied while my head went into limbo. It was ten minutes to seven. Ten minutes until the final ordeal. I touched a little pale lipstick to my cold mouth and ran a hand through my hair, then, wrapping my heavy black coat around me, I went out into the night.

*   *   *   *   *

The grass crunched frostily under my feet as I crossed the village green towards the single streetlight outside our inn. The curtains were drawn against the howling gale but light still glowed through the old, thick glass windows, and the sound of muffled voices could just be discerned from within. I braced myself, took a deep breath and walked inside.

They were all there, seated at an incongruous looking Formica-topped table beneath an old moth-eaten stag's head with Christmas baubles suspended, rather mockingly, from its antlers. A wood fire burned in the open grate and the air was heavy with the mingled scents of driftwood and cigarette smoke. I cleared my throat to indicate my arrival and they all looked over in my direction.

Yes, they were all there: the vicar and the two old women who had been to the funeral, comfortable now in the warmth with glasses of stout in their hands; silver-haired Doctor Mossom who had helped out in our hour of need and provided the death certificate; quiet Colin Armstrong, the local joiner, who had laboriously crafted the beautiful dark-oak coffin we had buried today, and the towering Bell brothers who had effortlessly carried the heavy stones up from the beach at the dead of night so that it wouldn't appear too light.

And, lastly, her golden hair glowing like polished gilt in the reflected firelight, curled up in her chair like a ginger cat grooming itself by the hearth, sat the light of my life, my darling, my Laura.

She looked up at me matter-of-factly as she smiled. "It all went according to plan then?"

"Yes, Darling," I replied, tears streaming from my eyes, "it all went according to plan. She's gone and you can come home!"

MEATBURGERS

When the girl with the big knockers asked him home for coffee it should have felt like hitting the jackpot. But it was only when she told him that her name was Fuchsia Saal that he finally threw his misgivings to the winds. And that was how Oliver Norville - poet, biographer and thick shit - found himself speeding through the night in the front seat of a cream-coloured MG, while his host sang loud and tunelessly and occasionally put both hands on the wheel.

But as dark country lanes flew past, and Oliver turned from bright green to deepest viridian, he consoled himself with the knowledge that he had just pulled off the literary coup of the century. For beside him sat the sole daughter and heir of the late, great Terence Saal - philosophical children's author, rampant vegetarian and dedicated disciple of Shaw. Saal, the preacher and shaper of young minds. Saal, the semi-recluse who had shut himself into his beloved country mansion with only his daughter. Saal, the stricken, who had been brutally murdered by persons unknown thirteen years earlier. Saal.

His passport to glory.

And he *should* have been ecstatic. The girl was delicious. She had the biggest pair of tits since Paula Page. She was his ticket to the big time. Quite frankly, perfection had never been so perfectly packaged. And yet...

He was bumped back to the present as the car careered through the towering gates of the Saal country estate. Stone eagles surveyed him with steely eyes as the car sped up the rutted drive. Overturned gargoyles leered from the darkness; waist-high grass hissed and gravel spat from beneath the MG's wheels as Fuchsia brought it to a screeching halt before the cracked marble steps that led up to the huge oak door.

They were here.

"Nice place," Oliver said as he climbed unsteadily out of the car, fighting the urge to turn around and bolt. "Stylish."

"Stinks," she replied, opening the door and ushering him inside.

"Right," said Oliver, as the musty smell of damp and rotting carpets delivered him a body-blow to the solar plexus. "See what you mean."

"Shhhh," she whispered, as the door and the last glimmer

of moonlight closed into the darkness behind her. "Don't let him know we're here."

Her voice was high with suppressed excitement and the warning bells that had been tolling all evening in Oliver's brain began to play a carillon. But it was too late, and soft hands were already dragging him in, while the dark and creaking house seemed to scream out in anger.

* * * * *

"Fuck me here or upstairs?" Fuchsia breathed in his ear, when she finally removed her limpet-lips from his, and taking his croak as a sign of assent, she led the way up a huge staircase into the even deeper gloom of the upper floors.

"Dark," he whispered, as he followed her up the winding flight, trying hard not to break his neck on the shreds of rotting carpet that still clung to each step. "No moon," he tried again as tiny clawed feet scurried away before them, and Fuchsia giggled in reply.

"Want one?" she asked, unbuttoning her skirt and then flinging her Aertex – they couldn't be, *could* they? – knickers into the darkness.

Limping up the treacherous stairs behind her luminous white behind and finding himself short of breath, he almost tumbled backwards into the hungry dark when she reached the top and whirled round to face him.

But her kiss was a glazier's suction-clamp and his clothes just seemed to melt away under her skilful fingers, and, lost to all that was pure, he threw himself willingly into the Abyss. (The man *is* a poet, after all.)

Oblivious to the fact that he was teetering on a rotten wooden step with a thirty foot drop behind him, he clumsily removed her top and then groped for the bra catch that would unleash her cantaloupian delights. Only to discover that there wasn't one and that her magnificent tits were contained in – wait for this – a vest. Which she obligingly removed for him.

And then what felt like a hundred tiny fingers were wrapping themselves around his bursting cock, guiding it towards where he wanted it to be, in spite of some dark thing's obvious disapproval that he was about to sink into paradise – you'll note that he had skilfully avoided using the word Heaven – when she suddenly broke away from him, skipping off into the algae-smelling darkness, chanting, "the library, the library" like a child's rope rhyme.

And he followed, of course. Although he felt suddenly vulnerable without her white-light body; and ever-so-slightly foolish with his cock bouncing in front of him like a nodding dog. (He wondered what they'd say at the Society of Authors if they ever found out about how he did his research.) But he still went on, following the tiny wraith that glimmered ahead of him, by now just a streak of blue-white on a greeny-black canvas that was trying to extinguish its light... "And mine?" he wondered aloud.

Then a door opened like a hidden hatch on a Ghost Train and swallowed her up and he was alone. Alone and naked in a dark and damp old house that made Miss Havisham's seem like Holiday Inn, and all the literary glories in the world did nothing to compensate for the scurrying sounds of hobgoblins, and the invisible eyes that watched and hated him.

It was the first time in his life that the thought of winning the Booker Prize was unable to bring a warm glow to his heart.

"I'm wet, I'm willing and I'm waiting for you," cried a voice which he hoped was hers. And the walls were damp and dead-fleshy to his touch, but the threatening darkness was pressing behind him, sodomising him forward. So he went on, when, suddenly, in the dull, dark and soundless hall, an opening – a maw? – materialised under his furtive fingers and he sighed with relief.

It was just a door. A plain and ordinary door. Well, ordinary for this place, at any rate. Not the sort of fitting that came as standard with your average Barratt-hutch or anything like that. A big, Gothic monstrosity hewn out of tree trunks, but just a door nevertheless.

But by now he had entered the big room and seen her and was lost. She was lying naked on a huge maple desk, theatrically lit by a single shaft of silver moonlight, her body a sculpture in pure white silk.

But it was the deep, dark patch between her legs that beckoned to him and drew him to her like a fly to a honeyed trap. And he went, his cock pulsating like a harp-string, eager to pay her in the coin she desired, enveloped into her vampire's kiss, just as the first shards of dawn broke over the hills and the house became still once more.

* * * * *

The sun was shining brightly through the fly-spattered panes when she finally acknowledged satisfaction, and Oliver was about to sink into grateful slumber on the desktop when she kissed him and galloped off through a shadowy arch crying, "Hungry?"

Strip-lights flickered into life to reveal a clean and expensively fitted kitchen nestling anachronistically amidst the decay of the house, and, acknowledging defeat, Oliver stretched himself and proceeded to survey the Great Man's library while she cooked breakfast. And that was when it hit him. Smack between the eyes. For although the room was what he had expected – oak panels, huge baronial fireplace and shelves to the ceiling on three walls – there was something missing. Something very important. Yep, you guessed it.

Books.

Empty shelves like Old Mother Hubbard's surrounded him. Even the dusty spider's webs were derelict, their predatory tenants moved on in search of fresh carrion. Only dust and a few discarded undergarments of Fuchsia's adorned the shelves' oaken lengths, and the two steely eyes that had haunted him all night bored into Oliver's skull and hated him for seeing it.

And at last he found their owner. For there, above the huge fireplace, greened and damp with mildew, hung the Great Man himself, his large angry eyes bulging with fury at the naked figure who sat on his desk like a plucked and oven-ready turkey.

"It's only a portrait, you fool," Oliver told himself, but covered his genitals anyway. "Only a fucking portrait!"

But the Great Man's eyes seemed to glow in defiance at the mere suggestion of this, and, in an effort to break the crucifying stare, Oliver called, "What happened to all the books?"

"Burnt," she replied.

But the shelves were intact, no sign of violence. "They were in storage?" he tried again, and could feel the eyes laughing at his bewilderment.

"No."

"But how..."

"*I* burnt them."

"You?"

"On the lawn. In box loads. Took three weeks and ruined the turf."

"But..."

"Hate books," she laughed. "Daddy used to always read his to me. Called me his sounding board. Read his books to me when I was still in nappies. So when I inherited I took them all out to the lawn and burnt them. Was lovely."

"It *must* have been quite a drag being the only daughter of the world's most famous children's author," Oliver said patronisingly.

"Shitty," she agreed, unperturbed. "Hated it. Hated books.

Hated him."

"Check," said Oliver politely.

"Was going to kill me," she continued, hacking at an onion, "because of my tits."

Mad as a hatter, thought Oliver, ever-fast on the uptake – you see the type of material we have to work with here – Mad as a fucking hatter.

"I was going to be thirteen," she went on, dropping the diced onion into the spitting fat, "and he was throwing a big party for me. He only ever let people come to his stuffy old house on my birthdays. He invited his 'young readers' and the press to take photographs. And he ordered me a new white frock and little white socks and white ribbons for my hair. But the dress wouldn't fasten because of my tits. They were too big, and suddenly I wasn't his little girl any more. So he took me out to the woods at the edge of the estate to kill me. But he was interrupted. He saw some poachers or someone. Chased them and never came back. They must have killed him, I suppose. But you know all this.

"I had to manage the party all by myself. I wore a tiny skirt and a tight sweater, and threw out all the nut pastes and honey cakes and served meat. And I flirted with all the journalists and told them about how I hated books, but they didn't print it and I was carted off to stay with my aunt, and this place was shut up. But by the time I was twenty-one he was officially dead and I inherited. So I burnt his books and let his house rot. And I cook meat in his library and fuck men on his desk and he doesn't like it but can't do anything about it. So now he knows how I felt."

She lapsed into silence again, lifting food from pan to plate, and, to break what he thought was an uncomfortable silence, Oliver called, "What's cooking?"

"Burgers," she replied, walking naked through the doorway, her pendulous breasts swaying over the laden tray. "I'm obsessed with them. I made a huge batch of them in the food processor for the kids to eat on my birthday and it was the first time I'd eaten meat and I thought it was sensational. And I still can't get sick of eating burgers."

"But where did you get all that meat from?" asked Oliver, reaching for his plate. "There wouldn't have been any in the house, surely?"

"Oh, Daddy provided that," she said matter-of-factly. "Mustard?"

But Oliver had suddenly lost his appetite.

SHHHHHH!

The trouble with living in London flats nowadays is that you never can tell when you're going to be lumbered with a corpse at twenty past ten in the evening. Like Mr Crispin was.

And, strangely enough, it had all begun just five minutes earlier as one of those perfectly ordinary everyday neighbourly exchanges, with Mr Crispin tactfully suggesting to the young lout downstairs that it might be a really tip-top idea to put a sock in that damned row he was making, and the aforementioned lout rejecting Mr C's plan of action with a succinct two-word negative. A perfectly commonplace flat-dwellers' conversation, and, of course, whacking the yobbo one on the head with a handy cast-iron doorstop was just the natural conclusion to their neighbourly tête-à-tête, the consequences of which were now lying at Mr Crispin's feet.

But progress *had* been made, and the noise – which had been the initial cause of their impromptu get-together – being quickly silenced by a sharp blow to the CD system, it now left only the tiresome red tape of getting rid of the evidence to be dealt with before Mr Crispin could get back upstairs and finish making his mother's cocoa.

There was the temptation to just leave well enough alone and let someone else to attend to all the discovery and disposal bit, of course, but it might be *weeks* before that happened, and Mother had been quite intolerable last summer when the drains blocked and the smell had driven her – and everyone who came into contact with her – to distraction.

So, mentally saying goodbye to his planned pre-bedtime hour with his new definitives, our hero sighed and decided that it was time that he gave his neighbour a friendly lift.

There were only two flats on the lower floor – Mr C and his mother occupying the upper – and as Number 1 was lying in a heap at his feet and Number 2 was in darkness, Mr Crispin estimated that the coast was clear for a quick disposal. With an involuntary grunt of distaste, he bent and picked up Number 1 by the feet and began to haul him out to the corridor, just as the street door swung silently open on noiseless hinges.

Ironically, Mr Crispin had, himself, oiled those very hinges not more than a week ago, because the nocturnal comings and goings of Number 1 were disturbing Mother, and now it seemed that his efforts in the interest of a quiet life were backfiring somewhat. However, he had little imagined that he would be dragging a lifeless human down his hall, unaware that someone was watching his every move, the 'someone' in question being 'Number 2' to Mr Crispin and his mother, Lola to her friends and "Would you look at *that!*" to the ticket sellers at the tube station.

Now, at this point in our story Lola would have been obliged to advertise her presence by screaming her pretty little head off, but as we're telling it like it is we can abandon lip service to the genre and go for realism. Lola raised her eyebrows, and, finally seeing her, Mr Crispin – who wasn't totally without style himself, in spite of living with his mother and collecting stamps – managed to aspire to a reasonable impersonation of his normal voice and murmur, "Oh, I *am* sorry. I do hope I'm not in your way?"

"Not at all," purred Lola in a voice that could melt hearts at fifty feet – or paint at fifty yards, if you're of an uncharitable disposition. "It's so nice to see someone carrying out a service for the community."

"The community?" Mr Crispin gulped, trying not to look down the valley of milk-white cleavage that was spread cinemascopically before his eyes.

"Why, yes," she replied, all Sugar Kane Kowalczyk. "The quiet is so precious in the city, don't you think? It's so nice to see someone preserving it." Then she added thoughtfully, "Tell me, do you have a script or are you just improvising?"

Mr Crispin was totally at a loss for words at this point, but he managed to convey that he was, in fact, following the latter course, and Lola smiled encouragingly.

"A post-modernist. How quaint," she intoned huskily. "Have you thought of the canal?"

"The canal?"

"Yes, a very dark and dangerous footpath with poor lights. Not the sort of place for a lady to frequent at night. Terribly lonely, you know. A man might slip and die there, in all that dark water. So sad, don't you think?"

Mr Crispin didn't, actually, but as a tiny tear was trickling down Lola's porcelain cheek he proffered his handkerchief and pretended that he did.

"Why don't you run along down to the water," she whispered, playing seductively with a button on her dress, "while I fix up a little something..."

* * * * *

Outside, it had begun to pelt down rain, and the very sight of it made Arnott Halliday scowl. For Constable Halliday was not a happy man this fine evening; not only had he forfeited his night off at very short notice *and* been paired up with Joe You-See-To-It-Arnott-Lad Anderson, but – worst of all – he had only just succeeded in spearing his first sweet and sour pork ball on the blunt prongs of his white plastic fork when the radio had crackled into life and asked him to check out an anonymous tip-off about somebody dumping a body in the canal.

"I ask you," Arnott had grumbled, throwing down his fork in disgust, "who in their right mind would be out dumping bodies in this bleeding downpour?"

But the dull metallic rattle of the incessant raindrops pitter-pattering on the car roof was his only reply, and if Anderson actually *did* say, "You see to it, Arnott, lad," the other had pretended not to hear.

*   *   *   *   *

Lola was feeling just a little bit mean when the doorbell rang. She had been standing by the window watching the flashing lights on the police cars down by the canal, and it seemed a really low trick to just stand by and let that sweet little rabbity-faced man from upstairs get caught in the act of disposing of his *habeas corpus* after he'd so obligingly got rid of that noisy tyke from next door.

Still, she told her conscience, it wasn't as if he hadn't killed the man in the first place, after all, and, more importantly, there *was* the little mater of the radio. For if Mr Crispin would insist on rising at six every morning to listen to "Farm Progress" on his mother's old wireless set at a volume fit to waken the dead, he didn't really give a person much choice, did he? And really, she asked herself, wasn't being free of that torture worth just a little bit of bad conscience now and again?

Yes, Lola thought, it certainly was, and setting her lovely face into a small sad smile, she went to answer her door.

*   *   *   *   *

Mr Crispin had to wipe a bitter tear from his eye as he surveyed the aftermath of the holocaust that had devastated his stamp collection. Old Halliday had known how to drive a hard bargain, and the fat toad was going to gloat insufferably at their Philatelic Club meetings for at least the next six months to come.

Still, he thought ruefully, the damage could be made good eventually, and it was a far, far better thing than landing in the clink over slapping that little thug in Number 1.

It *was* a shame, though, he conceded as his conscience administered a sharp jab to his posterior end, that they'd had to frame the pretty little girl downstairs, but since it had almost certainly been she who'd brought the gendarmes into the picture in the first place she could jolly well take what was coming to her.

Well, yes, alright, he admitted, he *could* have left her out of it altogether, but there *was* the little matter of all those bluesy saxophone records that she insisted on playing well into the small hours, night after night. Surely it was worth a little bad conscience to be free of that torture for life.

Yes, sighed Mr Crispin as he reached for his tweezers, it most certainly was, and, bending over his stamp album, he began to savour the unfamiliar sensation of perfect peace.

* * * * *

So perfect a picture of domestic bliss did he make revelling in the sheer joy of his own contentment that it seems almost cruel to chronicle the entry of a promotion-hungry young CID man who was, at that moment, going through the contents of Lola's apartment with the proverbial fine-tooth comb. Or, to record that at any minute he would discover the bloody cast-iron doorstop, neatly wrapped in the conveniently monogrammed handkerchief that Mr C had proffered to Lola in a mad moment of misplaced chivalry...

* * * * *

Of course, it was all purely circumstantial and didn't actually *prove* anything, but the jury, who were an easily-led bunch of oiks from Beckenham Junction, had swallowed the prosecution's lurid reconstruction of wilful, premeditated murder, hook, line and sinker, and took exactly ten minutes to give their seal of approval to a fifteen year sojourn at Her Majesty's Holiday Camp, Brixton. Worse, they even decided that poor little Lola deserved four years in Holloway as a consolation prize for her role as accessory, which really was the cherry on the parfait.

Still, that's just the way the cookie crumbles, and the whole sorry affair was, as the local broadsheet put it, "just one of those all-too-common domestic tragedies of metropolitan life." And under normal circumstances, Mr Crispin's "disgrace" would have broken his poor old mother's heart and forced her to slink quietly out of the neighbourhood. But, as it happened, dear old Mrs C was over-the-moon at getting rid of all of her nasty noisy neighbours in one fell swoop, and had no intention of going anywhere.

After all, she could always take Clarence his stamp album when she went to visit him in the prison, and there was nothing to stop him listening to his wretched farm programme in his cell, now was there?

Yes, Mother Crispin sighed happily, wasn't it wonderful the

way that just one little phone call had solved *all* her problems so perfectly.

BAD GIRLS

CLAIRE

Of course, it wasn't always like this here. Before the war, there were gardens and grand pianos and even a ballroom on the first floor; all palms and mirrors and Bohemian crystal chandeliers. All gone now.

Mind you, things were bad for us even before Hitler and his damned Luftwaffe, but when we came back afterwards all the fight had gone out of Leyland and he just wilted like a papier mâché toy that had been left out in the rain. By the time ten years had gone by, he was an invalid in a wheelchair, living like a hermit in the downstairs morning room, and he was dead well before the dawn of the next decade.

Anyway, the long and the short of it is that he left me without a penny, just this old house and a couple of useless share certificates. But the lawyer I had was good, son of the original old fool who had managed Leyland's affairs for god knows how many years. "Property," he told me patronisingly, oblivious to the fact that Leyland used to sit him on his knee and read him fairy tales, "property is an asset more valuable than silver or gold. And this old house could make you a very rich woman indeed."

"And where, exactly, will I live if I sell?" I asked. "Some dreary flat in Bayswater?"

He flashed me his crocodile smile. "Oh no. Not *sell*, my dear lady, *renovate*."

And so he convinced me. I mortgaged the whole place and turned it into flats. Luxury apartments, he called them. They even left me the old morning room and one of the finer drawing rooms for myself.

And I have to give credit where credit's due – the gamble paid off. A dozen rents come in every month and I've cleared the mortgage and the lawyer's substantial management fee, plus I still have a few coppers left to put away for a rainy day. But it's all so sordid, and, well, *middle class*. In the first conversion they made the flats quite big and left the garden intact, but five years ago we "remodelled," squeezed in extra rooms and tarred over the lawns and tennis court to make a car park.

And that was how Claire came back into my life. The wan nine-year-old off-spring of some dreadful school master's daughter who worked from her apartment all day, talking on the telephone and typing. "I really want to be there while Claire's growing up," the woman had the nerve to tell me. "Childhood is so brief, don't you think?" It would have been funny if it wasn't so tragic.

So Claire, a poor lost soul, invisible and ignored, mooned around like a wraith, talking to her doll and answering back in its voice. Sometimes their conversations were so intricate that it seemed like there actually were two of them out there. And, of course, there were no other children for miles, so she just flitted about like a lonesome ghost, carrying out her conversations with her imaginary friends, her pale, lifeless blonde hair trailing in the breeze behind her, her long white dresses shapeless, like shrouds.

She made me shiver.

I told the lawyer that I wanted rid of both mother and child, but he said that it couldn't be done until their lease expired. He actually found my distaste *amusing* and suggested that I should befriend the little apparition. "You could be company for each other," he smirked, but I was having none of that. Leyland was the one who liked children. I didn't. Always had one on his knee or was whispering with one in corners.

I put up with the children, of course. I owed that to Leyland. He had been the glue that held my life together when Father was threatening to lock me up in a convent and throw away the key. As if what Cynthia went and did with her father's straight razor was my fault. She wrote a note to me in blood on the white bathroom tiles, but they never let me see it. All I saw was her pale little foot on the black and white encaustic flooring and the seeping dark burgundy puddle before a policeman dragged me away screaming. We had only *kissed*. It wasn't as if she could have had my babies.

But Father just stormed and Mother took to her bed and wouldn't let anyone in except the maid with the decanter, and it seemed certain that I would be sentenced to life in some gloomy Irish nunnery when Leyland stepped in and took me back out into the sunshine.

He was the junior partner in Father's firm, although he was nearer Father's age than mine, but he offered to marry me and it seemed like an olive branch, so I grasped at it with both hands. I hadn't been looking forward to doing my wifely duties with him but was prepared to think of England for his sake, but he told me quietly in the taxicab to the boat train that there would be none of 'that'. "We're not like that, you and me," he whispered gently in my ear. "There can be others if we employ discretion. But you and I, we are going to be the greatest of friends." And we were. For fifteen glorious years, until Claire came along.

For me, there was no-one after poor Cynthia, but Leyland had a steady stream of them. He was a good, kind man. He never hurt them and always had a ready supply of sweets and toys if they cried. Sometimes it was imperceptible, a finger stealthily slipped under knicker-elastic while he rocked a child on his knee. Even the nannies and mothers were oblivious. Other times it was walks in the garden and then there was more elaborate stroking. But he always obtained his own relief in the privacy of his rooms.

Until Claire. A sickly little chit of girl sent to the coast with a nanny "for her health". If there were parents we never saw hide not hair of them during that windswept off-season fortnight at Hastings. Just the nanny flirting with the fisherboys on the pier, while the child trawled the beach, her long, pale hair like a Chinese funeral flag.

That was when Leyland fell in love.

They soon became firm friends, on the beach together building sandcastles, winning a rag doll for her at the coconut shy. And, of course, the nanny just handed her over every day without a backward glance. Letting the kind gentleman pet and stroke her charge as he would.

I watched it all like some dreadful road accident unravelling in slow motion. He was getting more and more audacious and taking foolish risks. But it was in the bathing hut that Thursday that she became emboldened enough to touch him back. And from then on it was a helter-skelter ride to disaster. She quickly learned how to do what he wanted done, and I sometimes had to wash the stickiness from her pale delft-coloured sundresses before we returned her to the nanny. But no lasting harm had been done until that final day, when he asked her if he could do what he had never dared to even imagine before, and she had given her consent.

To this day, he still comes to me in the dark hours, carrying her like an unstrung puppet, blood on his clothes, his face distraught. "She kept saying yes but then it hurt her and she saw the blood. And she started screaming and screaming. I only wanted her to be quiet. I didn't want to *hurt* her."

And after that we had no children in the house, until the war came and let us slip quietly away. But now my greed has brought this second Claire back to haunt me, whispering incessantly in tongues as she flits in the dark trees beyond the car park that I would not let them tear down.

In the purple twilight she's nothing more than a cut-paper silhouette, but I can still hear her – hear them – as they whisper and point their long thin fingers at me and accuse me with their maggot-rotted eyes.

But I don't understand how she's conjured her up. I buried that child so deep. So very, very deep...

POPPY

It was about the same time that she buried Poppy that Rachel began to keep all the lights on. Not that Poppy planned to give her any trouble, of course. At least, not then.

In fact, Rachel never knew quite why she kept all the lights blazing, she just felt better when she had their reassuring glow, that was all. And after a while she never even noticed they were there.

The neighbours did, of course, but it didn't really surprise them. Rachel and Barry's house – "The Rowans" it was called, although there was only one carbon monoxide-choked tree in the garden of the squat over ostentatious dwelling – was regarded as something of a joke in the locality, and the nightly illuminations were taken as just one more flaunting of the Voller's new-found wealth.

Anyway, that was the set up. Owner of South London building firm married daughter of civil servant; made a packet out of "property development" and built himself what he thought was a tasteful box on a handy access road for the South Circular. A little too handy, actually. Rachel had dutifully borne two off-spring: Jason, first-born son and heir conveniently packaged off to "a good school"; and Poppy, a lonely wraith of a girl mooning around the house wondering who her mother was.

So, the consequences were: Barry out minting in the coin; Rachel sipping Sauterne in the Wine Bar with her pals; Poppy out riding her BMX bike on the main road one minute, under the gigantic wheels of a Spanish mushroom and tomato truck the next. No more Poppy. For the present anyway.

*   *   *   *   *

It goes without saying that the funeral was a lavish affair and Poppy couldn't have complained about the send-off her old man threw for her. Massive floral tributes, fantastic Daimler hearse, ten limousines and a Fortnum and Mason's buffet lunch. Real class.

And Rachel. Rachel was *superb*. She played her role of Grieving Mother to perfection. First at the funeral, where she turned every male head, clad in a sheath-like black Jaeger dress, completely austere, except for a single silk poppy like a splash of blood on her beautifully sculpted left breast; and, for *ne plus ultra,* a discreet but just discernable tear running down her cheek.

Then each week at the monumental black marble gravestone, which would have looked more at home at Forest Lawn that West Norwood Municipal Cemetery, changing withered blooms for fresh and delicately brushing the cobwebs from the colour photograph of Poppy specially printed onto an enamel plaque.

Poppy had never had so much attention in her life.

Of course, it didn't last, as any of the over-painted designer-denim-clad tabbies at the Wine Bar could have told you. And did, frequently, if you happened to be there. But to give Rachel her due, she managed almost a full year before her performances at the cemetery became less regular.

At first it was nothing to shout about. Some moss left on the side of the towering ebony stone because she'd just painted her nails. Then sometimes it was two weeks between visits, sometimes three. Once she didn't have time to call in at the florists for fresh flowers so she skipped them. In fact, she began to skip them quite often.

"After all," she told herself wryly, "Poppy won't be any the wiser."

* * * * *

Now, in life, Poppy had always been a patient child, twelve years experience of her mother had taught her that much, but lying in a hole in the ground with nothing to do all day tends to have a strange effect on people and it gave Poppy plenty of time for thinking and reflecting.

In fact, her collective thoughts amounted to the decision that maybe her mother could do with a little sorting out. So when the flowers on her tombstone had been neglected for five whole weeks she decided that opportunity had knocked.

She would pay her mother a little visit.

*   *   *   *   *

As luck would have it – depending, of course, on whose side you're on – Rachel was all on her lonesome that night. Barry had phoned to say that he would be "late" three and half hours ago, and she suspected that she wouldn't see him before the pubs closed. Not bargaining on her daughter's impromptu call, she resigned herself to the remains of lunchtime's Blue Nun and the copy of *Pet Semetary* that she'd slipped into her trolley at Safeways.

So she was quite engrossed when the awful scraping sound started.

Now Poppy had never been a particularly smart kid, but on this occasion you've got to give her credit. This was real House of Usher stuff, and even the brightly-lit modern house and incessant roar of traffic outside did nothing to dampen the atmosphere she was creating.

Rachel's book slithered from her hands and her heart paused when she saw who – or perhaps *what* – was running its very dirty fingernails down the glass of her very expensive plate-glass window. It certainly left Stephen King on the starter's block.

She watched as Poppy's talon-like nails cut a neat circle out of the glass and her bloodless white hand reached in and snapped off the special security catch. "Absolutely unbreakable" the salesman had said. Then the window flew open and the smoky November night poured in.

Mother and daughter faced each other across the room.

Poppy smiled. It wasn't a pretty sight. A delicate crumb of soil tumbled from her mouth as she spoke. One word.

"Mummy."

The Blue Nun bottle that was staining the deep-pile hand-woven Chinese carpet gurgled on unnoticed. The cold wind blew dead leaves and litter into the room. A four foot china tiger – one of Rachel's favourite ornaments – was caught by the icy gale and toppled, shattering into a thousand pieces.

Then Poppy bobbed gently through the open casement like an animated fairy in a pastry commercial, a tiny flutter of skin-flakes and soil raining from the folds of her rucked and flounced grave dress.

Rachel turned and fled.

Slamming door after door behind her, she sped out of the brightly-lit house into the drive and leapt into the driving seat of her Suzuki SUV. She wasted precious seconds as she rummaged for the keys, then the comforting leather fob fell into her hands and she jammed the cold metal into the ignition.

Then, as the motor roared into life, the passenger-side door opened.

If she'd had time to think about it she couldn't have done it, but as it happened, she didn't, so she could, and Poppy went sprawling onto the gravel, reeling from the impact of her mother's ferocious blow.

Wrenching the car into gear, Rachel churned gravel, scraped the gatepost and ruined her tyres as she screeched out onto the main road and was swallowed immediately into the river of honking headlamps.

Oblivious to their wrath she sped on, her foot jammed down on the accelerator, and it was only when the needle began to creep past ninety that she finally noticed the hand wrapped round the shaft of her left wing mirror.

Her last impressions were jumbled. Poppy's face grinning like a demented goblin; the sound of tearing metal as the Suzuki's bonnet was flung upwards; the windscreen cascading into her lap like falling cherry blossom; then *Splat!* as they say in all the best comics.

*   *   *   *   *

So it was yet another lavish funeral, but Baz, who was getting to be quite a dab hand, went and stole the show by turning up with his 'secretary'. In fact, he grabbed so much of the limelight that nobody even noticed Rachel's reproduction Tudor Coffinette as it was lowered down into Poppy's domain.

No-one except Poppy, that is.

And Poppy was feeling rather pleased with herself. Daddy wasn't going to be bringing Mummy many flowers, that was for sure, so Mummy was going to have to learn how to lie alone in the dark, day in and day out, just like Poppy did. Yes, Poppy would have her revenge. Nothing could go wrong now.

At least, so Poppy thought.

The trouble was it didn't work out like that.

Rachel was a social animal, a mixer, and there was Ian and John, the Falklands heroes from the East Rise; and the Marchmont girls from the big mausoleum; and the Brockbanks who had all gone together when the gas boiler exploded. All told, she hardly ever saw the inside of her own coffin.

Come to think of it, she didn't see much of Poppy either. Poor Poppy. Talk about down the snake at square ninety-nine.

THE HUT

We stayed at the hut every weekend, summer and winter alike, but it wasn't until the September of my thirteenth year that Sindy came to me there. Came on the evening tide, when the setting sun turned all the shallows to blood, her red bathing suit glorious against the last vestiges of the fiery sky.

Going to the hut was our family ritual. Every Friday evening Dad would load up the Cortina with tinned food and blankets and packets of teabags and Bachelor's soup. Then, together, we would take Mum's wheelchair up to the open door and lift her inside, packing the chair in the boot, then, me scrambling into the back seat with all the blankets and provisions and stuff, we'd be off, six o'clock on the dot, starting out on the long drive to Dungeness.

Mum never went out in the Cortina except to go the hut. In fact, she never went out at all when we were at home, not even to the garden when it was warm. Dad got the shopping and did the housework, mowed the lawn and cleaned the car. Pretty much everything, in fact, except the cooking. I did that, except for when we went to the hut and he made me thick and sweet hot chocolate from tinned evaporated milk.

Looking back, they were my golden days. But we weren't what you'd call a happy family. Mum's illness made her snappy and bad tempered, and though Dad could be sweet to me, he was like a polite stranger most of the time. But we all managed to get along, and, of course, we had the hut.

The hut was our own secret, very private place. Life was relaxed and tranquil there. Even Mum became placid, and Dad and I used to comb the beach for driftwood while she sat on the porch and read her magazines, or in the summer, she sometimes came down the ramp we'd built for her chair, and sat looking out across the water towards France, a distant, far-away smile on her face.

Some of the huts along the beach sat in little clusters, like villages, but ours stood alone out on the headland north of the lighthouse. It could be quite bleak in winter, but on summer weekends, when the water was a sheet of Azure blue glass, it was the most beautiful place on earth. Not that our weekends were a time for slacking, of course, and there were still chores to be done and routines to be strictly followed. We had no electricity and no running water, so it was my job to fill the lamps with oil, then go out with the little cart Dad had made from old pram-wheels and top-up our barrel from the standpipe at the end of the lane, then bump it back down to the kitchen before I started on breakfast.

Meals were simple, though: cereal with tinned milk, tinned fruit and tinned meat, packets of soup that I heated up on the tiny gas ring, bread that was curling at the edges by Sunday night, when we packed up and headed back home. There was a shop up at the lighthouse, but I don't remember ever going there. Mostly we just kept to ourselves. Except when Uncle Louis came to visit.

Mum's brother, Louis, was the only person who ever came out to the hut, and, although he was always kind to me and called me Honey, I could never warm to him. He came down about once a month from town, where he had a flat above his accountancy practice, his long white American car incongruous amongst the dunes and couch grass slopes of the east downs, his city suits unsuitable for the sandy scrubland around the hut.

I don't think that Dad was any too keen on Louis, either, and he tended to shy away from him, but, thankfully, his visits were never long. Sometimes he would only stay long enough to share a mug of tea with Mum, and the two of them would whisper and giggle together out on the porch like conspirators. Other times he would stay the night. But the sea air always exhausted me and I would fall asleep after my drinking chocolate, and I can only remember Dad's grim face and Louis' satisfied smirk before it would be the next morning and he would be gone.

And that was our life; functional, well-oiled and dull. It was no small wonder, then, that when Sindy arrived on the evening tide that hot September night that my whole world would be turned inside-out.

I expected considerable resistance to her presence, but Mum and Dad appeared to be indifferent to her, and Louis didn't even see her, as we ran laughing through the hut, leaving wet footprints behind us, and clattered into my room to change.

I had never really had a friend before and was overcome with a sudden shyness as Sindy pulled off her wet bathing suit and dropped it onto the linoleum at her feet, where it lay, damp and brooding, like a puddle of blood.

"Come on, slowcoach, you'll freeze," she laughed, throwing a towel to me, "get dried!" And, as I quickly wriggled out of my now cold and sticky costume, I stared at her naked body in the yellow lamplight. I was white and sinewy, long and straight, like a stick of rock that had had all the colour sucked out of it, but Sindy was golden and undulating, like the dunes on a warm afternoon.

"Get dressed, pervert!" Sindy grinned, pulling a nightshirt over her head and breaking my stare, and I slid guiltily into my pyjamas as Dad came in with my beaker of drinking chocolate.

"Drink up!" he said with a friendly wink, slipping quickly back out of the door, oblivious to the fact that he'd completely ignored my friend.

"I'm so sorry, Sindy," I started, proffering my mug, "he mustn't have realised that you were here. Do you want to share mine?"

But Sindy shook her head and put a finger to her soft lips. "It's OK, we don't need their chocolate. Put it down on the window sill and let's just listen."

It seemed an odd request, but she took the cup firmly from my hands and led me to the door, where we lay down together and pressed our eyes to the crack of light that shone through, projecting an image of what was going on next door like the screen of a pin-hole camera.

Louis was standing by the stove, playing with something metallic while he toasted his fat backside. I could hear the driftwood I had gathered that afternoon crackle and spit.

"Well, last drop tonight, Georgie-boy. Nice juicy boatload to bring in and then your work here is done."

"About bloody time too," another voice said querulously.

Mum's. "Another year of playing spastic mother-of-the-year would have sent me round the bloody bend."

Dad crossed our line of vision with storm lanterns in his hands. "The *girl!*" he said reprovingly, but Louis only laughed.

"She'll be in Lullabyland by now. Those pills would knock out a horse."

"Probably have done, too..." Dad muttered.

Then the creak of Mum's chair. "Come on, let's get this done, I can't wait to get to Paris."

"Just a minute," Dad's voice again, authoritative now. "Money first."

Louis' bulk fills the crack. "Money, George? You want money? I seem to recall that you've had rather a lot of that already, down at the track. I don't think you'll be seeing any more."

Dad pushes into the narrow screen of our magic lantern show, crowding the fat uncle. "We had a *deal,* Louis. Ten years picking up the shipments and hiding your sister for you. That pays off my debt. Now I want my kiss-off money."

Louis laughed, fingering his toy. "A deal? You're far too

trusting, Georgie-boy. Didn't you realise that I'd just dump you when your usefulness had run its course?"

"Why not give him the brat," Mum's voice cuts into the tension with a brittle laugh. "You can unleash all your darkest fantasies when you've got her all to yourself, Georgie."

"*For God's sake...*" Dad breathed.

"Don't be getting all moral on me now, Georgie-boy," Louis sneered, suddenly striking Dad across the face and knocking him to the floor.

Dad let out a fast breath, like a hiss, backing away from Louis and his brass knuckles as Mum came into view. Walking. *Without* her chair. "For God's sake, Louis, we haven't got all night. Deal with this idiot while I get the girl."

Louis started to laugh again, when suddenly there was an ear-splitting retort and he seemed to fly backwards into the air, smashing into the protesting hut wall like a sack of coal hurled down cellar steps.

Mum's voice again, only an octave higher this time.

"George, *no*. I always liked you, George. He forced me to..." Then another explosion and her face falls against the crack in the door, blocking the scenario with its hideous slack-eyed grin.

I felt Sindy's hand lead me quickly back to the bed as Mum's body was shoved roughly to one side and the door dragged open. Dad stood silhouetted in the lit rectangle, like the one-armed-man in *The Fugitive*, the old shotgun we kept behind the kitchen larder in his hand.

"It's all right," I heard him saying as he leaned over me, stroking my face with his bloody butcher's hands, "it's all right. They're gone, they're gone, it's just you and me now, babe." And I really wanted to throw my arms around him and bury my face in his shoulder and cry 'Daddy, Daddy, Daddy,' but all I could feel was the hard thing that pressed against me, and came between us.

"Dad," I whispered, as Sindy fingered the sharp darning scissors from Mum's work basket, "I'm alone. I've always been alone."

And I sank back and let Sindy plunge her crocodile scissors straight into his heart.

If you have enjoyed this book please post a review to your favourite online bookstore today

BAD GIRLS

Printed in Great Britain
by Amazon